Shh! Bears Sleeping

by David Martin

pictures by Steve Johnson and Lou Fancher

VIKING

VIKING

An imprint of Penguin Random House LLC

375 Hudson Street

New York, New York 10014

First published in the United States of America by Viking,

an imprint of Penguin Random House LLC, 2016

LIBRARY OF CONGRESS CATALOGING-IN-PUBLICATION DATA IS AVAILABLE

ISBN 978-0-670-01718-8

Text is set in FCaslon Twelve ITC Std

The artwork for this book was rendered with oil on paper prepared with gesso

Manufactured in China

1   3   5   7   9   10   8   6   4   2

For Judy and for Nabby
—D. M.

For Robin
—S. J. and L. F.

Shh, bears sleeping

But not for long

Winter is over

Says a bluebird's song

Spring is here

Bees hum

Bears wake up

Here they come

Skinny bears

With winter hungries

Gobble food

To fill up tummies

Berries, honey

Maybe bees

Bugs and grubs

In rotten trees

Cubs frolic   All day

Climb trees   Run and play

Follow momma

Stop and eat

Chase fish

Splash feet

Spring summer fall

All day long

Bears grow big

Bears grow strong

But in the fall

When leaves turn red

Bears know soon

It's time for bed

Comes winter

Comes snow

Bears are ready

Bears go

In their den

Warm and deep

Winter is time

For bears to sleep

Bears pile

In a heap

Bears yawn

And fall asleep

Squirrels play

Play all day

Rabbits hide

And run away

But bears sleep

In winter deep

In a cave

In a heap

Snowflakes swirl

Snowflakes fall

Deep white

Covers all

Under moon

With icy ring

Owls hoot

Coyotes sing

But no sound

Not a peep

From bears

Deep asleep

Night and day

Day and night

Through winter cold

And winter light

And winter wind

And ice and snow

While blizzards storm

Bears lay low

Underground

Beneath the snow

Fast, fast

Fast asleep

Wake up, bears

Winter is going

Warming sun

No more snowing

Wake up! Wake up!

It's warm at last

Spring is coming

Coming fast

Bears wiggle

Bears shake

Winter over

Bears awake

And here they come!

Shh, Bear Facts

THE BEARS in this story are called American black bears. But there are other kinds of bears, too: polar bears, grizzlies and Kodiaks, Asiatic black bears, giant pandas, sun bears, and spectacled bears.

Bears are big, and they have big appetites; they aren't picky eaters. Some animals, like lions, eat only meat. They're called carnivores. Other animals, like deer, are vegetarians. They eat only plants, like grass and fruit. But most bears are omnivores. They eat anything that's food—bugs, grubs, apples, nuts, mice, fish, birdseed from bird feeders, garbage, anything! When they find a beehive full of honey, that's a treat. And if they gobble up a few bees at the same time, oh well, that's okay, too. In the fall, when apples are juicy and ripe, bears have a picnic. They eat the apples that have fallen onto the ground. Then they shake the trees to make more apples fall and climb the trees to pick the rest. Catching fish is trickier. Fish are fast, but bears are fast, too. They stand in rivers and grab the fish with their mouths or bat them out of the water with their front paws. Then they run over to get them. How fast are bears? They can run faster than most people can ride a bicycle. In the warm time of the year, in the spring and summer and fall, bears spend their time roaming the woods. Bears cubs, when they're small, look like roly-poly bundles of fur. They learn to hunt and climb trees while their mothers watch to make sure they are safe.

When it's wintertime black bears go to sleep—not just for the night, but for the whole winter. They sleep for about one hundred days. It's a special kind of really deep sleep called winter lethargy. How do they sleep all winter? First, they have to eat a lot during the summer and fall so that they get fat. That's how they store up enough energy in their bodies so they don't have to eat in the winter. Then, when it turns cold, they find a den, maybe in a cave or in a hollow under fallen trees, where they are protected from rain and snow. Of course their thick fur coats keep them warm, too. In this story momma bear is sleeping with her cubs. She will do this for two winters. After that they're off on their own. And when winter returns, they'll find their own dens.

Most people think bears hibernate in the winter. But they don't. Some animals, like toads and groundhogs and bats and snakes, are true hibernaters. During the winter they hardly breathe. They're out cold—unconscious—for the whole winter. If you found a toad hibernating, you'd probably think it was dead, even though in the spring it will wake up and hop around. But if you found a bear in the winter, you'd know it was really just asleep. You would see it breathing very slowly. You might even see it move a little. On warm days, sometimes bears wake up and walk around a little, and then go back to sleep.

Mother bears might not be very awake during the winter, but believe it or not, that's when they have their babies. Usually in February, in the den, in the dark, while she's sleeping, her teeny little babies are born. There might be one or two, or sometimes three. Right away they wiggle themselves up onto their mother's chest, snuggle into her warm hair, and

nurse on her milk. Then in the spring they are ready to explore the world. It would be exciting to see one. But even though baby bears look like cuddly teddy bears, they are really strong wild animals. And remember, where there's a baby bear, there's sure to be a momma bear close by. So be careful!